LEGEND

Great Bear Rainforest

Grizzly bear helicopter flight

• • • • • • Grizzly bear walk/swim route

International boundary

Alberta

British Columbia

GREAT
BEAR
RAINFOREST

VANCOUVER
ISLAND

Vancouver

CANADA

US

Victoria

PACIFIC OCEAN

Washington

The Great Grizzlies Go Home

JUDY HILGEMANN

HARBOUR PUBLISHING

In the little island town of Alert Bay, life was usually a peaceful mix of sun and rain, work and school, family and friends. One September day, things were a little different.

Two unexpected visitors were on their way. They came by water, but not on the ferry. Their paws made good paddles, and their strong muscles pulled them through currents and tides.

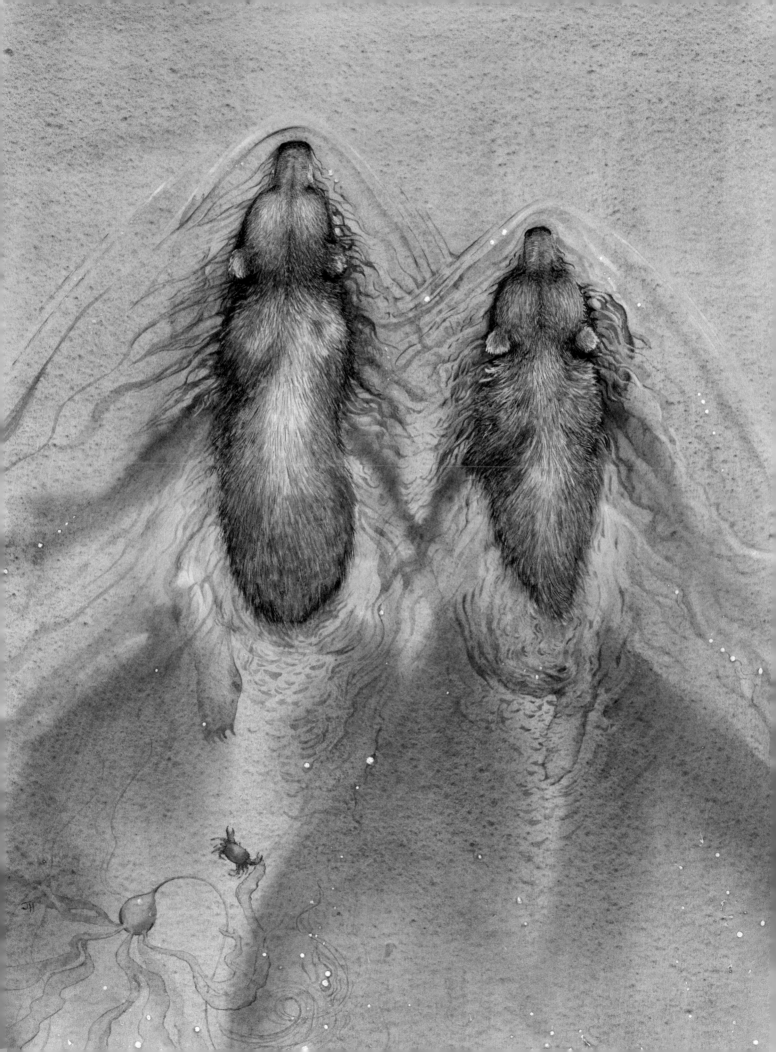

The two big bears clambered out of the ocean
onto a rocky beach. Shaking the salt water from
their thick fur, they set off to explore.

The bears' noses led them to juicy cranberries and
crunchy grasses in a swamp behind town.

At the end of the day they
sat and watched the sun set
behind Vancouver Island.

Early in the morning the bears snuffled through
the quiet streets and nibbled at gardens.

The bears lumbered along the beach in front of
town, snacking on grassy roots and tiny shore crabs.
They used their long claws to dig and hunt.

The next day the bears wandered through backyards and
feasted on fruit trees until they were "plum full."
Neighbours asked each other, "Did you see them?"
"Did you get a photo?" No one had ever seen
a grizzly bear on Cormorant Island before.

Conservation officers set bear traps to catch the grizzlies without hurting them. The bears were more interested in a sweet smoky smell from a barbecue.

But after a few days the bears checked out the traps. When
they stepped into the big blue containers to investigate
the plum and salmon snacks, the trap door banged shut.

The conservation officers tranquilized the bears and moved
them to the airport. With the help of the helicopter pilot,
the officers placed the sleepy grizzlies on a large net.

Everyone was very happy to see the bears fly
back home. "Goodbye!" the schoolchildren called.
Now it was safe to play outside again.

The helicopter lowered the bears onto a soft grassy
bed beside the sea. The bears woke up and sniffed
the air. They padded into the forest as the thump-
thump-thumping of the helicopter faded away.

Grizzly Bear Facts

- About 15,000 grizzlies live in British Columbia.

- Grizzly bears are the largest members of the bear family in British Columbia. Males can weigh up to 500 kilograms— as much as 5 refrigerators!

- They can be dark or light brown and sometimes have blond tips on their fur.

- Grizzly bears have large muscles on their shoulders that look like a big hump.

- They can live to be 30 years old.

- Grizzlies can run very fast— faster than a racehorse— over a short distance.

- They have excellent eyesight, hearing and sense of smell.

- Coastal grizzly bears need a home range of 50–500 square kilometres per bear. That's somewhere between 7,000 and 70,000 soccer fields! Bears need such large areas to find enough food during the different seasons.

- Grizzlies are omnivores, which means they eat both plants and meat. Plants are their main food source.

- Coastal grizzly bears eat as many as 17 different types of berries.

- Cubs usually stay with their mothers for 2½ years.

- Grizzly bears live alone once they are adults.

- Grizzlies are an important part of the natural cycle of life. When bears drag dead salmon into the forest, the decomposing salmon bodies fertilize the soil. Bears eat other animals that are already dead and this helps clean up the environment. Bears dig up roots, mixing the soil and making it healthier. Bear droppings spread berry seeds and fertilize the land.

- Human settlements, activities, industry and roads all can threaten grizzly bears.

- Grizzly bears are important cultural figures among BC First Nations.

Hiking and Camping Safety

- Never feed bears or wildlife!
- Never hike alone. Always take an adult with you.
- Make noise so bears know you are there.
- Stay together in your group.
- Keep pets on a leash.
- Adults should carry bear spray and know how to use it.
- Don't camp in known bear habitat.
- Keep all food and toiletries in airtight containers and away from your tent.
- Cook and eat far away from your tent.
- Hang garbage and all food in a tree well away from your tent.

Bear Encounters

There might be a bear nearby if you see the following signs:

- Bear footprints or tracks
- Bear poop
- Rotten logs that are torn apart
- Trees with bear hair in the bark
- Scratch marks on trees
- Fresh digging for roots and grasses
- Chewed-up skunk cabbage plants

If you see a grizzly bear...

- Don't run!
- Back away slowly.
- Talk calmly to the bear in a low voice as you leave the area.

The Great Grizzlies' Adventure

N

W — E

S

Alaska

HAIDA GWAII

INSET

Ahta River

Broughton Island

Gilford Island

Queen Charlotte Strait

Malcolm Island

Sointula

Cormorant Island

Pearse Islands

Port McNeill

Alert Bay

Harbledown Island

Hanson Island

West Cracroft Island

Telegraph Cove

Robson Bight

Johnstone Strait

Vancouver Island